Elephant on Wheels

story by Alida McKay Thacher
pictures by Jerry Scott

based on sketches by Ted Schroeder

 GOLDEN PRESS
Western Publishing Company, Inc.
Racine, Wisconsin

Petunia was an elephant.
Her family loved her.
But she was not like other elephants.
You see, Petunia liked to roller skate!

She skated on her back feet.

She skated on her front feet.

She skated up steps.
She skated down steps.

She even skated between Father's legs.
This made him angry. Very angry.

"An elephant on skates!"
Father said.
"That is a very silly thing."

But Petunia kept skating.
She did a trick on one foot.

"What will our friends say?"
cried Brother.

Petunia just kept skating.
Around and around she skated.

"Elephants are heavy,"
said Mother. "They should walk.
They should not skate."

Petunia thought a minute.
"Most elephants don't skate," she said.
"They don't have skates. But *I* do!

"Besides," Petunia said,
"skating doesn't hurt anything."

"It hurts our floor," said Sister.

Petunia thought a little more.
"You are right," she said.
"Elephants should not skate . . .
in the house."
So she skated out the door.

Petunia's family sat down to talk.
"Something must be done," they said.
"We must stop Petunia.
She should not roller skate."

They thought and thought.

Then Father said, "I have a plan!
I will take Petunia's skates.
I will hide them in a secret place."

Everyone said this was a good plan.

So that is what Father did.
Petunia came home.
She took off her skates.

Father took the skates.

He put them in a secret place.

But the next day . . .

Petunia was on roller skates!

"That was a bad secret place,"
said Mother. "Petunia found her skates.
I will hide them. I will put them
in a *very* secret place."

So that is what Mother did.
Petunia came home.
She took off her skates.

Mother took the skates.
She put them
in a *very* secret place.

But the next day...

Petunia was *still* on roller skates!

"That was a bad secret place,"
said Brother. "I will hide her skates.
I will put them
in a *very, very* secret place."

So that is what Brother did.
Petunia came home.
She took off her skates.
Brother took the skates.

He put them
in a *very, very* secret place.

But, yes, the next day . . .

Petunia was on roller skates again!
Sister said, "You all have
very bad secret places.
Now *I* will hide Petunia's skates.
I will put them
in a *very, very, very* secret place."

So that is what Sister did.
Petunia came home.
She took off her skates.

Sister took the skates. She put them in a *very, very, very* secret place.

"Petunia will never find them," she said.

But—you guessed it!—the next day . . .

there was Petunia on skates again!

"Oh, no! Not *again!*"
her family cried.

"Petunia found her skates
in my secret place," said Father.

"Petunia found her skates
in my *very* secret place," said Mother.

"Petunia found her skates
in my *very, very* secret place,"
said Brother.

"But how could she find her skates
in *my* secret place?" said Sister.
"My secret place was *much* too secret!"

"Our plan did not work!"
said the family.

Petunia laughed.
"I have a plan, too," she said.

"Go to your secret places.
See what you find there."
They all went to their secret places.
And each one found something.
Each one found *four roller skates!*
They were surprised!

And a funny thing happened.
Father loved to skate.
So did Mother. So did Brother.
And so did Sister.

And do you know what?
They never again
told Petunia to stop skating.
They were busy skating, too!

Then they skated on their back feet.
They skated on their front feet.
They skated up steps and down steps.
They even skated around
one another's legs.

The family put on their skates.
"Now," said Petunia, "follow me!"
At first, the elephants skated
this way and that way.

But Petunia wasn't surprised.
She laughed.

"I couldn't find my skates," she said.
"You put them in secret places.
So each day I had to get new skates.
And now we *all* have skates!"

The family smiled.

"You can all roller skate,"
said Petunia. "You just have to try."